Dear Parents:

Congratulations! Your child is taking the first steps on an exciting journey. The destination? Independent reading!

STEP INTO READING® will help your child get there. The program offers five steps to reading success. Each step includes fun stories and colorful art or photographs. In addition to original fiction and books with favorite characters, there are Step into Reading Non-Fiction Readers, Phonics Readers and Boxed Sets, Sticker Readers, and Comic Readers—a complete literacy program with something to interest every child.

Learning to Read, Step by Step!

Ready to Read   Preschool–Kindergarten
• big type and easy words • rhyme and rhythm • picture clues
For children who know the alphabet and are eager to begin reading.

Reading with Help   Preschool–Grade 1
• basic vocabulary • short sentences • simple stories
For children who recognize familiar words and sound out new words with help.

Reading on Your Own   Grades 1–3
• engaging characters • easy-to-follow plots • popular topics
For children who are ready to read on their own.

Reading Paragraphs   Grades 2–3
• challenging vocabulary • short paragraphs • exciting stories
For newly independent readers who read simple sentences with confidence.

Ready for Chapters   Grades 2–4
• chapters • longer paragraphs • full-color art
For children who want to take the plunge into chapter books but still like colorful pictures.

STEP INTO READING® is designed to give every child a successful reading experience. The grade levels are only guides; children will progress through the steps at their own speed, developing confidence in their reading. The F&P Text Level on the back cover serves as another tool to help you choose the right book for your child.

Remember, a lifetime love of reading starts with a single step!

To Grampa Fred and Nancy,
who make a cloudy day sunny!

Copyright © 2019 by Tad Hills
All rights reserved. Published in the United States by Random House Children's Books,
a division of Penguin Random House LLC, New York.
Step into Reading, Random House, and the Random House colophon are registered
trademarks of Penguin Random House LLC.
Visit us on the Web!
StepIntoReading.com
rhcbooks.com
Educators and librarians, for a variety of teaching tools, visit us at RHTeachersLibrarians.com
Library of Congress Cataloging-in-Publication Data is available upon request.
ISBN 978-0-525-64493-4 (hardcover) — ISBN 978-0-525-64496-5 (ebook)
ISBN 978-0-525-64495-8 (lib. bdg.) — ISBN 978-0-525-64494-1 (paperback)
Printed in the United States of America
10 9 8 7 6 5 4 3 2 1
This book has been officially leveled by using the F&P Text Level Gradient™ Leveling System.

Rocket's Very Fine Day

Tad Hills

Random House 🏠 New York

"We are lucky
it is a sunny day,"
says Bella.

Rocket counts only
one cloud in the sky.

Rocket and Bella
play in the meadow
all morning.

They play hide-and-seek
in the tall grass.

Bella chases Rocket.

Rocket chases Bella.

They walk across logs.

They play fetch
until they are tired.

They rest and
count the clouds.

But now there are
too many clouds
to count.

It is not sunny
anymore.

Bella feels a raindrop.

Rocket feels

a raindrop, too.

Soon it is raining hard.

"Oh no!" cries Bella.
"I do not like
the rain."

Rocket and Bella
sit under a tree
to stay dry.

They watch the rain
come down.

"I do not like the
rain," says Bella.
"But I do like . . ."

"PUDDLES!"

Rocket and Bella splash
in big puddles.

They splash
in small puddles.

They splash
in deep puddles.

They splash in
muddy puddles.

The rain stops
and the sun
comes out.

They splash
some more!

When the sun sets,
they stop splashing
and they rest.

"We are lucky
it was a rainy day,"
says Bella.
"Yes, lucky indeed,"
Rocket agrees.